Miss Fannie's Hat

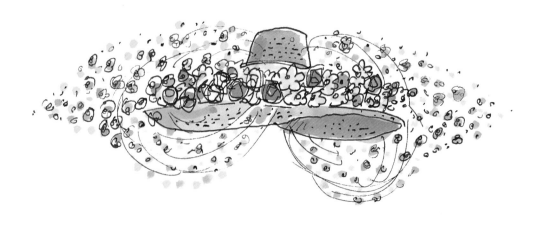

Written by Jan Karon

Illustrated by Toni Goffe

PUFFIN BOOKS

For my mother, Miss Wanda,
and in grateful memory of my grandmother,
Miss Fannie

PUFFIN BOOKS
Published by the Penguin Group
Penguin Putnam Books for Young Readers, 345 Hudson Street, New York, New York 10014, U.S.A.
Penguin Books Ltd, 27 Wrights Lane, London W8 5TZ, England
Penguin Books Australia Ltd, Ringwood, Victoria, Australia
Penguin Books Canada Ltd, 10 Alcorn Avenue, Toronto, Ontario, Canada M4V 3B2
Penguin Books (N.Z.) Ltd, 182-190 Wairau Road, Auckland 10, New Zealand

Penguin Books Ltd, Registered Offices: Harmondsworth, Middlesex, England

First published in the United States of America by Augsburg Fortress, 1998
Published by Puffin Books, a division of Penguin Putnam Books for Young Readers, 2001

7 9 10 8

Text copyright © Jan Karon, 1998
Illustrations copyright © Toni Goffe, 1998
All rights reserved

LIBRARY OF CONGRESS CATALOGING-IN-PUBLICATION DATA
Karon, Jan, date
Miss Fannie's hat / written by Jan Karon ; illustrated by Toni Goffe.
p. cm.
Summary: When ninety-nine-year-old Miss Fannie gives up her favorite pink straw hat with the roses,
to help raise money for her church, she receives an unexpected reward.
ISBN 0-14-056812-3
[1. Hats—Fiction. 2. Conduct of life—Fiction. 3. Old age—Fiction.] I. Goffe, Toni, ill. II. Title.
PZ7.K146 Mi 2001 [E]—dc21 00-062661

Puffin Books ISBN 0-14-056812-3

Printed in the United States of America

Miss Fannie has lots of hats.
And each one is her favorite.

3

When she wears her red felt with the big feather, she looks in the mirror and says, "I just love this hat!" And her friends at church say, "Miss Fannie, we just love that hat!"

When she wears her green velour with the fancy pin, she says, "I sure do love this hat!" And her Sunday school teacher says, "Miss Fannie, I sure do love that hat!"

But, when she wears her famous pink straw with silk roses, she always says:
"I *really* love this hat!"
And everyone else really loves it, too.

Miss Fannie is ninety-nine years old. And very small.
In fact, she's grown to be about the same size she was as a little girl.
Miss Fannie and her daughter, Miss Wanda, live together.
Miss Wanda makes breakfast every morning.
"Don't make me much breakfast," says Miss Fannie, sitting on the sofa in her robe.

Miss Wanda tries to mind, because Miss Fannie is her mama. But she forgets, and brings her a piece of sausage, buttered toast with jelly, a scrambled egg, and a cup of herb tea.

"Oh, my! That's way too much," Miss Fannie always says. But then she goes and eats it all up.

Every morning after breakfast, Miss Fannie reads her Bible. She has worn out three Bibles, reading them over and over. Her very favorite verse is, "With God, all things are possible."

Every Saturday, Miss Wanda washes Miss Fannie's hair.

Miss Fannie takes off her robe and stands around in her slip, looking very tiny. Then she gets on a stool and sticks her head in the sink.

Miss Wanda runs the warm water and puts the shampoo on her mama's head and scrubs until it lathers up. Then she scrubs some more.

"That feels good!" says Miss Fannie.

After she washes her mama's hair, Miss Wanda rolls it up in tight little curls all over her head.

The curlers are real hard to sleep in, but Miss Fannie doesn't care one bit. She knows that when she goes to church the next day, she will look beautiful.

On Sunday morning, Miss Fannie puts on a pretty dress and high-heel shoes. She puts on earrings and necklaces and lipstick and blusher and powder.

Next, Miss Wanda combs out her mama's hair, which is all nice and soft and gray, like the feathers of a dove.

Then finally, after all that fussing with her hair, she goes and hides it under a hat!

Miss Fannie has three black hats, two red hats, one green hat, two white hats, two navy hats, three beige hats, one brown hat, and the famous pink straw with roses.

Because she never wears the same one twice in a row, some people think she has a whole closet full of hats.

Which, of course, she does.

One Sunday, Miss Fannie's handsome young preacher came up to her and said, "Miss Fannie, would you kindly give us one of your beautiful hats? It will go in the auction to fix up the church in time for Easter."

That same day, Miss Wanda helped her mama get out her hats and put them on the bed and the dressing table.

Then Miss Fannie closed her bedroom door.

"Lord," she said aloud, "I'd appreciate it if you'd help me make the best choice." She always talked to the Lord as if He was right there.

Miss Fannie walked around the room and looked at each one of her hats.

The green velour with the fancy pin was very, very old, and still very beautiful. During the terrible flood of 1916, she had crossed the swollen river on a ferry to visit her mother and father. As she stood at the rail, holding on to her beautiful hat, a house had floated by, almost close enough to touch.

And over there was her wide-brimmed felt with the gleaming black feather.

Ha! That feather had come from the tail of a hawk that was trying to kill her hens and biddies. She had grabbed the hawk around the neck, and before you could say, "doodley squat" that hawk would never bother her chickens again!

Then Miss Fannie picked up the hat made of soft, brown velvet, and stroked it. It had always reminded her of Flower, her grandmother's cow.

When Miss Fannie was just seven years old, she had started milking the brown, velvety-soft Flower. Each evening, she carried the milk to the spring in a bucket, and set it in the icy water to keep cool. Later, her mama would pour the milk into a churn and Miss Fannie would churn it into butter just like you buy in the store, except better.

She realized that each one of her hats was like a friend. And each one brought back special memories.

Finally, Miss Fannie came to her most favorite hat of all: the pink straw with silk roses. She had worn it every Easter Sunday for thirty-five years, and it always made her feel brand-new, like Easter itself. But she wasn't the only one who thought it was special.

Everyone at church looked for her pink hat on Easter Sunday just as they looked for the tulips and daffodils to bloom in the spring.

Miss Fannie took the pink straw out of its round box and put it on, even though she was wearing her oldest housedress with the torn pocket.

She looked in the mirror and sighed.

In her heart she did not want to give her hat away.

Not at all.

She took a deep breath and repeated her favorite Bible verse.

As she placed the hat back in its round box, she said, "You know, this hat really could raise a lot of money!"

As she put the lid on the box, she said, "Maybe it could help fix our old pipe organ!"

As she tied the string around the lid, she said, "Why, it could probably mend the crack in the church bell, or put on a whole new roof!"

Suddenly, she discovered she was very, very excited.

At the church auction, the handsome young preacher held up the pink hat with roses and looked around. "What am I bid for Miss Fannie's famous hat?"

The bidding took off lickety-split. At last, here was something more exciting to bid on than a set of kitchen canisters or an umbrella stand.

Bang! went the gavel.

"Sold to the lady in the front row!"

The lady in the front row gave the preacher a check and seemed very, very pleased with herself.

"That's a lot of money!" exclaimed Miss Wanda, who was impressed.

Miss Fannie clapped her hands. It was enough to *really* get things fixed around here!

She knew that she would not miss her favorite hat one bit. But she did wonder which hat she would wear on Easter morning.

On Easter Sunday, Miss Fannie got up very early.

She sat on the side of her bed, and took the curlers out of her hair.

Although she thought and thought, she didn't have the slightest idea which hat she would wear.

Her red felt with the big feather was too hot!

Her green velour with the fancy pin was too wintery!

And there was no use to even think about the pink straw, which, of course, would have been just right.

When it was time to leave for church, Miss Fannie looked beautiful.

She was wearing her best dress, which was the color of pale green apples. She was also wearing her best jewelry, her best gloves, and a white corsage.

"It's time to go!" said Miss Fannie, picking up her cane and taking Miss Wanda's arm.

Miss Wanda could not believe her eyes.

Her mama was going out the door without wearing any hat at all!

When they arrived at church, Miss Fannie couldn't believe *her* eyes.

28

On either side of the freshly painted church, someone had planted beds of glorious pink roses.

Pink roses were also planted along the walkway, under the stained glass windows, and in front of the old fence by the street.

"Oh, Mama!" said Miss Wanda. "It looks just like your pink hat!"

The handsome young preacher greeted them on the steps and gave each one a big hug. "We hope you're pleased, Miss Fannie! We were able to patch the bell and fix the organ. And your beautiful hat made it possible to buy all these roses!"

As Miss Fannie laughed with delight, they didn't see an old woman at all. What they saw was a young girl, with hair as soft as the feathers of a dove.

Now, when people pass the little white church, they think they're seeing a garden of dazzling pink roses.

But what they're really seeing is Miss Fannie's hat. And it will always, always be her favorite.